We're All Friends Here

Nancy Wilcox Richards

illustrated by
Tom Goldsmith

Scholastic Canada Ltd.
Toronto New York London Auckland Sydney
Mexico City New Delhi Hong Kong Buenos Aires

Scholastic Canada Ltd.
604 King Street West, Toronto, Ontario M5V 1E1, Canada

Scholastic Inc.
557 Broadway, New York, NY 10012, USA

Scholastic Australia Pty Limited
PO Box 579, Gosford, NSW 2250, Australia

Scholastic New Zealand Limited
Private Bag 94407, Botany, Manukau 2163, New Zealand

Scholastic Children's Books
Euston House, 24 Eversholt Street, London NW1 1DB, UK

www.scholastic.ca

The art in this book is traditional ink brush drawing with watercolour washes.

Library and Archives Canada Cataloguing in Publication

Richards, Nancy Wilcox, 1958-, author
We're all friends here / Nancy Wilcox Richards ; illustrated
by Tom Goldsmith.

ISBN 978-1-4431-2832-2 (pbk.)

I. Goldsmith, Tom, illustrator II. Title.

PS8585.I184W47 2014   jC813'.54   C2014-902063-5

6 5 4 3 2 1   Printed in Malaysia 108   14 15 16 17 18

*For the Catidian Place Girls, wonderful friends who are
always here for me. Namaste!*
— N.W.R.

To Gord, Emily and Linda. For everything.
— T.G.

Arthur Leevy bugged me in nursery school. He bothered me in Kindergarten. And now I'm stuck with him in grade one.

Our teacher, Ms Nowe, said, "Sonny and Arthur, you sit at this table."

So now Arthur sits right beside me. He scatters his stuff everywhere. He always loses his pencils.

And he wiggles the desk. A lot. So I did my printing on my lap today. But Ms Nowe told me it was messy and she knows I can do better. Thanks to Arthur, I had to start all over again!

When Ms Nowe came over to help Arthur, he smirked and stuck his tongue out at me! So I stuck my tongue out back at him. But Ms Nowe only saw me.

She said, "Sonny, back to work."
"It's not fair," I tried to explain. "Arthur started it."
But she was not listening to me. Why does
Arthur always get more attention?

Finally, it was snack time! I knew
my mom packed one of her special
double-fudge brownies. But it wasn't in my
lunchbox.

That's when I looked over at Arthur.
He was licking his lips, and they were
covered in chocolate!

When I told Ms Nowe, she said, "Sonny, we're all friends here. I'm sure it was an accident."

Then she asked Arthur to share his cookies with me. Except they had raisins, and I don't like raisins.

We had gym in the afternoon. I was all set to race against Arthur, and win.

Mr. Fernandez yelled, "Ready, set, go!"

I took one step and . . . splat!

Then I saw the problem: Arthur's sweatshirt was tangled around my feet.

"No fair!" I yelled. But Arthur was halfway down the gym. He didn't even care that my knee was bleeding.

Guess who sits beside me on the bus?
Every day. Arthur always hogs the seat.
He makes rude noises and whistles and
sings. But mostly he tells long stories,
the grosser the better.

I've told Debbie, the bus
driver, that I want to change seats.
She always says, "But you and
Artie are good for each other."

In nursery school, the teacher thought Sonny Marshall was perfect. In kindergarten, the teacher said he was a ray of sunshine. Sonny never ever gets in trouble.

Sonny sits right beside me. He lines up his pencils in a neat row. He hardly ever uses his eraser. Sometimes he doesn't even look at the page, but he can still print in a straight line.

Today I had to erase so hard that I tore a hole in my paper. That wiggled the table. Sonny got mad because he had to do his printing all over again.

Ms Nowe came to look at my work and caught Sonny sticking out his tongue at me. When I concentrate, I know I stick my tongue out. Sonny must have thought I was sticking it out at him! Then he was even madder at me for getting him in trouble.

I erased three holes in my paper and there were black smudges all over.

Ms Nowe said, "You can finish this tonight at home, Arthur."

So then I had extra homework!

Finally, it was snack time, and I had a brownie! I gobbled it up in one bite.

Next thing I knew, Sonny was saying that I ate HIS brownie. It's not MY fault we both have red lunchboxes.

Then Ms Nowe made me give Sonny an oatmeal-raisin cookie. He said raisins are yucky but they're my favourite.

21

I was looking forward to gym all day. I pulled off my sweatshirt and lined up beside Sonny. He loves to race almost as much as I do. He is fast, but I'm even faster.

When Mr. Fernandez shouted, "Ready, set, go!" I took off. Sonny was not even close.

But then I looked back to wave and saw him in a heap on the floor.

That's when I noticed my sweatshirt under him. There was blood running down his knee and he looked upset.

My dad picked me up for a dentist appointment today. I told him I'd rather take the bus but he said we'd be late.

The car ride was quiet. I didn't even feel like singing. And my dad was not too interested in my story about Sonny's bloody knee. The drive to the dentist took forever.

Arthur had to go to the dentist today.
Before he left, he said sorry for tripping
me with his sweatshirt.
Now I have the bus seat all to myself.
I can read my comic and no one will bug me.
Except . . . It's no fun. And it's way too quiet.

The bus ride home takes forever. When I tell Debbie the bus ride is boring, she says to remember that tomorrow when Arthur is back.

On our way home, I tell my dad that I can't wait for school tomorrow. I'm going to tell Sonny all about getting my tooth pulled. And all the blood. I'll even show him a cool way to whistle with a missing tooth.

Sonny's going to love it. I just know it.